Grease Monster

Jerome Frank

 pencil

ISBN 978-93-5667-724-1
© Jerome Frank 2023

Published in India 2023 by Pencil

A brand of

One Point Six Technologies Pvt. Ltd.
Unit no. 26, Ground Floor, Building A1,
Wadala Truck Terminal Road,
Near Post Office, Antop Hill, Mumbai - 400037
E connect@thepencilapp.com
W www.thepencilapp.com

All rights reserved worldwide

No part of this publication may be reproduced, stored in or introduced into a retrieval system, or transmitted, in any form, or by any means (electronic, mechanical, photocopying, recording, or otherwise), without the prior written permission of the Publisher. Any person who commits an unauthorized act in relation to this publication can be liable to criminal prosecution and civil claims for damages.

DISCLAIMER: *This is a work of fiction. Names, characters, places, events and incidents are the products of the author's imagination. The opinions expressed in this book do not seek to reflect the views of the Publisher.*

Author biography

Jerome Frank is an artist, singer/songwriter and author who lives in Central Falls, RI. The 29-year-old author is currently writing books and creating scripts for upcoming movie ideas with his sister who works as a film producer. The author Jerome Frank currently has music available in all stores. The young artist/author uses Ditto Music as a distributor. If you are interested in listening to his upcoming music, please come check for Jerome frank and Frank Legree on www.Stationhead.com. The author's music is available on all streaming services and was recently playlisted by Spotify in 2021. The song 'Like You' was selected and featured in Emerging: The Hotlist in, December 2021. If you are a fan of this most recent piece of literature created by Jerome Frank, please stay tuned for more to come! Thank you for reading.

CONTENTS

Prologue

The streets of Fall River were silent, the moon was full and the sky was covered in stars radiating the dark summer night with a dim light. The city felt almost like a ghost town when the sun went down, no one was seen walking around past midnight. President ave. being one of the busiest Intersections in the city had no cars vacant except for one, and in the lot, on that very Road, there was a McDonald's. Suddenly Far off in the distance on the star-filled horizon, a green beam of light drew in closer, and closer. The closer it got the brighter the light began to glow. The unknown object was heading straight for the Restaurant. Daryl slammed open the back door of the McDonald's restaurant, he was taking out the garbage and was the only worker on the floor. He was also the only maintenance man the store had. The owners had hired Daryl to work by himself and clean the store overnight."Fucking pigs make such goddamn messes," said the old man as he staggered forward. 'Sick and tired of this shit, I'm too old for this." Daryl wore a blue button-up and was a white older man, he was a stocky type of fellow. Daryl appeared to be in his early 60's. The older man's hair was of course, completely gray. The heavy-set maintenance man came to a stop and decided to light up a cigarette, as he walked closer to the dumpster a beam of green light was closing in like a meteorite of some sort. It was coming from the sky at the speed of light. As Daryl approached the fenced-in grease storage unit, the light in the sky became overwhelmingly green, just as the poor old man realized something was coming his way a glowing object flew smack into Daryl's back. This random force caused the poor man to let out a howl of pain, as he flew smack into the grease bin and knocked it over. The blast from the sky had so much impact that it knocked him out, the glowing object slowed down but not enough to prevent someone from being knocked unconscious. As Daryl Lay on the ground, the grease started to cover his whole body, and the glowing light began to glow for a moment. Suddenly it began to heat up, the grease was bubbling somehow. The liquid almost seemed like it now had life in it, like a nasty sludge it began to clump together, and the temps began to rise, almost cooking Daryl alive. Shocked by the pain he awoke from his unexpected knockout. Daryl lay in a gigantic puddle of grease. His eyes were nearly blinded by the spill and coughing because he swallowed so much grease."Fuck!! It fucking burns!!!" Screamed Daryl as the grease glowed brighter. Something strange had been done to the liquid from the green glowing rock. As he tried to move it almost seemed like his skin was melting off. Daryl let out a more intense howl. The pain was too much to bear. His whole hand was melting away, all that could be seen was bone as the liquid was traveling down his arm. The grease almost seemed to be taking over his whole body, even eating away his bones. The pained maintenance man let out a blood-curdling scream "Oh god, please make this stop!!! What's happening to me!" screamed Daryl as the glob of Grease began to enter his mouth. As the grease took him over it was eating him alive. The liquid somehow appeared to be changing Daryl's genetic structure to grease. He screamed and screamed some more, the pain was too much to bear that he was shaking on the ground nearly having a seizure of some sort. Daryl began to crawl but he was dissolving by the second. His skin began to crackle off. His flesh now exposed looked like dried globs of grease as they fell off him. Soon enough after choking away on grease and blood, Daryl's face completely melted off, and he subdued himself to the grease. The liquid somehow devoured Daryl alive and melted him away, no longer was there a man laying there. Suddenly the goop rose, and the grease was beginning to resemble a mushy sludge. It began to harden, as it grew taller and taller. The freakish grease was somehow re-animated and brought to life. The man standing there was no longer Daryl. The maintenance man's body was now deteriorated and rotted away. He was now a monster. Now that the creature was alive, was Daryy dead or was he still somewhere in the monster's body?

Chapter 1 Marge

"I cannot wait until we get the hell out of here...this shit is crazy, I don't know If I'm going to make it." Said Sheila as she dropped another bun into the toaster and began to initiate the three sandwiches. "Just hold on girl we gonna be fine, we got like 3 hours of this bull shit then we outta here."Said Rosa as she threw some cheese on the remaining burgers and moved to the U.H.C cabinet. Sheila turned to the clock and rolled her eyes."I've been working here for eight years now. Time wants to sneak up on me when it comes to years, but when somebody wants a few hours to fly by it as fast as that...that new bitch walking over." Rosa quickly looked behind to see who Sheila was snickering at. It was Marge, The "new" employee. She'd just arrived on the floor, Marge has been working at the restaurant for a year and some change now."Yeah, look at her running to work. I can't believe she is still working here. After how many times she was late. That's a shame. Said Rosa as she slid another sandwich to the landing zone. Sheila glanced at the young woman for a moment; she was quite sweaty and almost out of breath. Marge's beautiful black hair was pulled back in a ponytail, her shirt wasn't tucked in and it was slightly unbuttoned around her chest. ."Hey! Marge" Said Sheila. Marge slowly turned around with a smile."Hey Sheila, how are you today?" Said Marge as she kept moving towards the staircase but slowed down for her co-worker."Oh, you know...same shit different day. Hey, can you do me a favor and grab me the shredded leaf in the fridge behind you?" Said Sheila as she looked at Marge with sincerity and smiled. Marge paused for a moment and turned for the fridge but remembered she hasn't clocked in yet, "Oh wait--' Marge stopped herself and turned around. "I'll be right back, I just gotta put my coat down and clock in."Sheila cocked her neck back"Late again huh??" She smirked and looked Marge up and down. Suddenly Rosa looked over too, Marge kept it moving and rushed away. "I don't like her, I'm sorry I just do not care for her. She's so weird." Said Sheila as she rushed around the table to grab the shredded leaf."Yeah, the younger girls tell me she's an oddball and nobody really talks to her. She's gay too." Said Rosa who huddled closer to talk about the young women's vibes which they felt were peculiar. " Ladies! I'm missing a Mcchicken?" Shouted Janet the store manager, she was old, short, and in one of her cranky moods yet again.

It was a nice day in the city of Fall River, a calm peaceful type of afternoon. It was around 4:15 PM as Marge clocked in to begin her shift at McDonald's. She'd felt Okay when she first walked in but on her way to put her coat downstairs, she overheard her co-workers talking about her. Her feelings were completely flipped soon as she heard what Sheila and Rosa said about her. Slowly she walked over to the two managers on the floor, Richard and Janet. Richard was tall and flamingly gay, and the young manager was also very slender. Janet was a short older woman in her fifties, she wore glasses, and her teeth were jacked up. Since McDonald's was her life career choice, she had no dental plan. Janet's looks perfectly matched her personality. While Richard was busy handling a child's ice cream, Janet glared over waiting for Marge."Hi Janet, Where would you like me to be today?' Marge had a feeling of nervousness quivering her whole body. She was praying Janet wasn't going to make her filter once again. The whole entire process is quite annoying; you're dealing with old hot oil that you have to bring outside in a heavy canister with a cap on it. To top it off you have to put on a shiny apron with enormous gloves. The job is usually done by a man but Janet insists that Marge does the filtering in exchange for her being late so much. A cruel punishment made for a girl her size. Janet smiled for a moment and then said "You're filtering the vats today." Marge cringed inside, The boys brought up the oil for you, so there's no need to go downstairs. It's 4:16, I want them all changed by 7:30. I mean it, I want it done fast." Said Janet with a stern tone. "Oh, I feel sorry for you." Said Richard as he gently tapped Marge's arm and laughed. It wasn't a shock but Marge felt infuriated. She wanted to have an outburst and cause a scene. She wanted to shove the filtering rod up where the sun don't shine, but she maintained her composure and headed to put the machine together. After two hours of filtering, Marge finished pouring some more hot grease into the storage unit and stopped outside by the dumpster to sneak in a brief cigarette break. She was beyond tired, her back was killing her and she was on edge just seeing a Rat-run by her feet when she first arrived. The storage unit was well kept by the maintenance man Daryl most of the time, but for the past couple of days, it was getting messy. Marge leaned against a busted fridge and smoked her cigarette. For a brief moment, she was happy to have a moment to think, Marge was under a lot of stress at home. Her brother and she were constantly fighting. Charles had disagreements about her lifestyle. He didn't like that Marge was bisexual. Charles and Marge were forced to live with one another when her mother passed away due to cancer 2 years before.'Ma, I miss you each and every day of my life...This just doesn't make sense to me, it just isn't fair...I wish this was a dream...why can't this just be a dream...' Thought Marge as she took another drag. In a timely fashion, Marge put her cigarette out and exited the messy storage area, when a random figure jolted her with fear. Her co-worker Tracey was rushing in to dump some trash and the two almost had a collision. Tracey was a gorgeous brunette. Her eyes were blue; she had rosy cheeks and the sexiest lips covered in pink lip gloss. Marge stopped and lost herself for a moment, something about her made her so wet. All Marge could think about was eating out another woman; she was an all-time whore when it came to women. Men? Not so much."Geeze, you came out of nowhere." Marge collected herself and moved out of the way as Tracey giggled and threw the trash into the dumpster."I'm sorry, I didn't mean to scare you. She looked Marge up and down with kindness in her eyes. "You gotta light?" She asked as she grabbed her back pockets checking for one of her own. Marge snapped back into reality and responded, "Yes I do." she locked eyes with Tracey for a moment and quickly looked away to look for her lighter, she passed it to her and watched her spark it. The way she looked in Marge's eyes made her wonder if she was into girls too. There was someone seductive lurking behind her innocent smile. Marge wanted to know who was hiding inside the cute new girl. "So you like working here so far?" Asked Marge as she took her lighter from Tracey's hand. "So far, I kind of like working here. I mean I don't really know how to make all the sandwiches yet...but I'm learning." Said Tracey as she smiled and puffed on her cigarette some more."Don't worry, everyone goes through that. You'll get it eventually, trust me." Marge smiled back to reassure her cute co-worker. "Thanks, I see you on the table and I'm just thinking, I wish I could be that fast...Janet makes me feel so stressed out whenever she's on the clock. Is she always so mean?? I feel like I'm working with a completely different woman from the interview." Marge laughed at Tracey's frustration and said, "Almost everyone feels that way! That's funny...I thought she was the sweetest lady until I tried to call out of work. Richard picked up the phone and all I could hear was her flipping out in the background, then she got on the phone and asked me why? I'm sorry, but it was beautiful outside and I didn't really want to work. I was honestly just trying to go to the beach. So I lied and made up something..." "Good to know." Said a random voice that cut through the brief moment of silence like a sharp blade. The voice came from somewhere behind the two ladies. Tracey quickly poked out her cigarette in a panic; automatically as Marge turned around she knew it was Janet in the flesh as she stepped from around the corner by the drive-thru."Oh, what's this? Smoking cigarettes while you're both on my time??" Janet looked at the two ladies almost waiting for some sort of response. Tracey looked at Marge and then looked at Janet. "I'm sorry--" Said Tracey, who Janet rudely interrupted."Unless you ask me for a cigarette break, there is no smoking allowed," She then glared over at Marge. "Marge, you've got three vats to go and it's almost 7:30. You need to hurry up. I want to get out of this store early tonight, now let's go." Said the short angry woman. 'Fucking bitch...I can't stand your ugly ass.' Thought Marge as she walked with Tracey toward Janet's direction, suddenly Janet stopped Marge and looked her straight in the eyes.``And I mean it Marge, with Daryl not showing up to work for the past couple of days we have to clean the store ourselves. I don't have time for this." Marge took a breath and responded calmly"Okay. It's just hard since you made me walk around when I forgot to lock the back door Janet rudely interrupted one more time and said, "I told you! And you keep forgetting, now you have to learn the hard way. Sorry honey." She smiled with her jagged teeth and headed inside with Tracey who was looking back at Marge as she rolled her eyes at Janet's behavior. At that moment Marge hated Janet even more. 'Why is she so mean?? I just don't get it.' Marge began to wonder if it was because she was so open about liking women. Could Janet not only be a super bitch as a manager but a homophobic super bitch of a person as well? It was beginning to eat at her the more she thought about it. So instead of overthinking, she shook it off and followed the two inside.

As the women stepped inside they were passed by men, women, and children coming from all directions. The restaurant was filled with a line of customers, it was dinnertime, and as usual tons upon tons of the same people would come on a regular basis. Even the old folks from the home down the road, Consistently the same people would come for their daily intake of McDonald's. Marge spotted so many hot women she wished she could talk to, but for some reason, she kept looking at Tracey. She had an hourglass shape; she had a nice personality and to top it off a beautiful face."Hey Marge, how are you?" Said a voice from behind, quickly she turned around to see Geo, Another co-worker. He was a short black man who was kind of cute, but quite strange."Geo! What's up, man?" She gave a warm smile and turned around to see Janet standing by the counter giving a look of impatience, instantly with one more look at her face, Marge's short moment of adoration was cut short.Finally after hours of walking back and Forth Marge finished up her filtering Job and cleaned up the machine. She then headed to look for Janet." Hey Marge?" Asked Sheila who was standing behind her "What's up Sheila?" Said Marge who was surprised she was talking to her. 'Oh god, here we go...time to play pretend.' thought Marge.Sheila was a pretty, young black woman who always had her weave-looking rite. She was quite urban and would tell anybody where to go in a hot minute. Generally, Marge would go after a girl like her but Sheila found lesbians weird. She was nice most of the time but everyone was afraid to say the wrong thing to her, even when she was talking smack about someone they like. Oddly Janet Was even afraid of the girl."Nothing much, you know, just being a bad bitch like usual. I was wondering if you smoke?" As Marge looked her straight in the eyes, she felt like Sheila was trying to stare into her soul, and when Marge looked her in the eyes she knew there was nothing sweet behind that stone-cold face, at all. "Yeah, I do actually. Why do you ask?" Asked Marge."Oh word, I just wanted to let you know my man got some fire on deck. If you ever need any, just let me know, okay?" Said Sheila who was trying at most to be that 'It girl.'"Oh, I'll be sure, to let you know. I have your number from when Janet had you call me the other day."Said Marge, then Sheila nodded and said "Okay, damn girl. Already got my number on your phone, what do you save it or something? You want to make sure you got me in your phone huh?"Sheila laughed briefly and looked Marge up and down with disgust, quickly Marge caught on to her accusation in such a passive manner and it began to tick her off. Marge tilted her head with a smile; she then rolled her eyes as she walked away. "Got to love Sheila." Whispered Geo who was just coming upstairs from the basement, slowly Marge turned around signaling 'Yeah right'. It was more like everyone has to love Sheila or she'll beat somebody's ass.' Thought Marge. Finally, after hours of work, the time favored most of all by the workers at Mcdonald's had now arrived. It was closing time in just five minutes. Marge was stuck doing the remainder of the dishes that were brought back throughout the night. She had a garbage bag with holes ripped in it placed over her to prevent water from splashing all over herself. There were only at least twenty more dishes left and the sooner Marge had them done, the sooner she and the crew had led the way on getting out of the hell hole she called work. 'Almost free…If I just hustle, we're out of here…' Thought Marge as she reached down for the bottle of degreaser under the sink. Noticing the bottle was empty she had no choice but to head for the maintenance aisle down in the basement. "Yo Margie." Said Geo, as he handed Marge a spatula. "What's up, Geo?" Asked Marge as she began to unclog the sink. "So Daryl's daughter is upfront, I overheard her talking with Janet…I guess the poor guy is really missing. "'What the hell could have possibly happened to the old fart?' Thought Marge as she walked straight away for a quick peek. The young woman was gorgeous, she had short bleach-blond hair and bright blue eyes. She was a petite kind of girl with a body truly like an hourglass. She was wearing a tank top and had a tattooed sleeve. You could see the worry in her eyes as she spoke with Janet and Richard who were available due to the low volume of customers."Poor thing she must be stressed out of her mind." Said Tracey who was trying to get a peak with Dorothy and Kelsey, two other workers who were on the floor as well. Dorothy was a short brunette girl with a little extra weight on her. Kelsey was a brown-haired short and petite kind of girl. "I know…all I heard was that when Janet and Richard showed up, the back door was unlocked and there was no sign of Daryl."Said, Kelsey. "That's so unlike him though. Something must be wrong, maybe someone kidnapped him?"Said Dorothy as she tried her hardest to get a quick glance."I could hear the worry in her voice while she was talking…she said she filed a police report Friday." Said, Geo. "I feel so bad…I mean I always thought Daryl was a mean cranky old dude, and I didn't talk to him…but still, this is all so scary. Where the heck could he be?" Said Marge as she tossed the degreaser into the garbage. "You know what? Daryl's daughter is kind of cute though, what do you think of her Marge? Does she look good?" Said Geo as he gently elbowed Marge. Kelsey looked at the both of them with an expression of confusion. "Why are you asking her if she thinks she's cute? She's a girl nimrod." Said, Kelsey. Marge began to feel slightly embarrassed; Geo basically just put her business out there to co-workers who barely knew anything about her. 'Might as well say it now' thought Marge. Quickly she looked to Tracey who was standing next to Dorothy who was already whispering in Kelsey's ear. "Wait what? REALLY?" Asked Kelsey as she giggled and looked at Marge."You're gay?"Asked Kelsey who was being a tad bit over the top. Suddenly everyone including Tracey looked over for Marge's answer. She didn't know what to say, Her brain almost felt like it stopped working for a moment. All Marge next started to feel was a cold bitterness and then a blast of empowerment. She wasn't in high school anymore; she didn't have to hide anymore if someone really wanted to know they were going to hear the truth. "Yes I like girls, and I like boys too. Is there a problem?" Said Marge with an attitude, as she looked at Kelsey with a fierce look in her eyes. Kelsey paused for a moment with a look of surprise and looked at Dorothy, Geo, and then Tracey and began to giggle.'Laugh all you want bitch, the only reason I haven't smacked the shit out of you is that you work with me.' Thought Marge "That's what's up, so you're bisexual?" Asked Geo with a smirk on his face. Marge began to hate the spotlight that was now beaming straight down on her, it was making her feel hot and uncomfortable. "What are you guys doing back there? There is work to be done around here; I don't want to see you standing around talking! Now let's go. Move!!" Shouted Janet who was still up front in one of her hot-tempered moods as usual. Before anyone could say anything else they all dispersed back to work and Marge quickly headed downstairs.

The basement was old and the floors were made of cement. The moment upon arrival both the fridge and freezer were direct across from one another. The ceiling was covered with tons of pipes; some were connected to the plumbing system. Random cords and tubes also shared the space on the ceiling as well, some were mainly connected to the soda dispensers upstairs. As Marge traveled deeper she passed all the isles that consisted of all the stock within the store. As she made her way to the maintenance section she couldn't help but notice the cracks in the ceiling. They all seem to have dried-up grease seeping from upstairs. The liquid was almost in a frozen state. 'Now that is disgusting, Janet needs to talk to that idiot who owns the store…cheap bastard…' thought Marge as she turned the corner. At that very moment a figure whipped around the corner, Marge's heart felt like it skipped a beat as her chest tightened and her breath grew short. "Oh my god!" Marge shouted in fear. To her surprise it was Jaylyn and Jessie, they were both alone in the maintenance aisle for some reason. "Jesus Marge, where the hell did you come from? I didn't even hear you come down the stairs." Said Jessie who was also startled by Marge. Jessie was another manager; she was a pretty blonde woman with sexy dark brown eyes. Jaylyn was an average-built kind of guy with dirty blonde hair and hazel eyes. "Yeesh, usually if someone like Janet is coming down you'll hear the stairs creak…you were really quiet when you walked down here." Said Jaylyn as he quickly began to search for something on the shelf beside him. "I'm sorry I just came to grab a bottle of degreaser…what are you guys doing down here all alone?" Said Marge as she smiled and looked at both her suspicious co-workers. "Oh um, I was just showing Jaylyn where the spray bottles are…" Said Jessie as she lost eye contact for a quick moment. "Oh, okay well can one of you just pass me the degreaser?" Asked Marge. Quickly Jaylyn grabbed the degreaser and passed it to Jessie who then passed it to

Marge. "Kay Marge see you upstairs." Said Jessie with a smile on her face. Marge nodded and headed back for the dishes upstairs. As she looked once more at the ceiling, something strange caught her attention and she couldn't shake it off. The very spot she looked at on the ceiling no longer had grease oozing out. Everything was completely clear of grease that appeared to be frozen in time. It just didn't make sense. Where could it have gone? There were no signs of it being on the floor, it was almost as if it was sucked back up into the ceiling. "He-hey you guys?" Asked Marge as she stopped dead in her tracks. Jessie and Jaylyn approached her from behind and came to a stop. "Yeah, Marge?" Asked Jessie. "Um, did any of you notice the grease seeping from the cracks just a few moments ago?" Asked Marge who was feeling confusion at its finest. "What? Ha-ha…what are you talking about? There was never grease seeping from the ceiling."'Impossible…' Thought Marge. She knew what she saw, and the fact that it "magically" disappeared just didn't make sense. "I-I just could have sworn…you know what, never mind." Said Marge as she began to shake it all off and forget about it. "You feel okay Marge?" Asked Jaylyn who had a look of concern but also a smirk on his face. "Yeah, you look a little confused, are you sure you're alright? I mean you're seeing things that aren't there." Said Jessie who was smiling now. "I'm good, I'm good…Just forget about it." Marge then backed away and headed back upstairs.

Chapter 2 Joan

"Where could you possibly be…what happened to you Dad?" Asked Joan as she stared at a picture on her nightstand of her and her father Daryl. It was Tuesday morning and she was finally crawling out of bed after hitting the snooze button for the fourth time. Slowly she dragged herself to the bathroom and began to get ready to start the day; she needed to head to the police station to check up on the officer she had spoken with the night before. She didn't care that the cops told her to leave it up to them to investigate. Joan kept in mind that Officer Thomas said to give him a call if she needed anything. What Joan needed was answers, she was going to find out the truth. Joan wanted to see if she could accompany Officer Thomas's investigation. After an hour of preparation, Joan finally put her gold studs in her ears. She then grabbed printouts of her dad that said 'Missing person' below his picture. Joan then headed out the door. As Joan drove down the road on her blue Harley motorcycle her stomach began to groan, mentally she felt disgusted and worried. Eating was the last thing on her mind. The fact that her dad hadn't come home or even called, told her that something was wrong. It was completely unlike him to not even call. As she drove down President Avenue she had a change of mind. Quickly she pulled into the driveway of McDonald's and decided to stop for coffee and breakfast. Joan quickly walked towards the restaurant while her mind took her somewhere else. She kept being overwhelmed with a sense of fear for her dad's sake. All Joan wanted to know was if her father was okay. Suddenly a car came speeding out of nowhere in Joan's direction. She let out a scream of horror when the car stopped just inches before striking her. "Jesus Christ!!!! What is wrong with you? You almost killed me!" Screamed Joan as she stared at the driver behind the wheel of the car. A Woman with black hair in a McDonald's uniform poked her head out of the vehicle with a look of shock. "Oh my god! I am so sorry! Are you okay?" Asked the girl who was shaking in fear. "How the hell did you not see me!" shouted Joan. "Look I know who you are…I'm sorry. I know you're going through a lot, let me make it up to you and I'll buy your meal alright?" Said the woman who was nodding and waiting for Joan to Agree. "No, it's fine. Just watch where the hell you're going next time." Said Joan as she began to walk away and head inside. "Wait, please! I'm sorry, all right? Let me make it up to you." Said the girl as she pulled over into a parking space. Joan immediately rushed for the bathroom, the stress she just experienced outside was overbearing and she needed to be alone for a moment.

Upon entering the lady's room she walked to an empty stall and made sure she locked it. 'Stupid bitch almost ran me over! She wants to claim she knows me. She doesn't know me! Who the hell is she?' Thought Joan as she wiped tears that began to pour from her eyes. After a few moments, she collected herself and left the stall. Suddenly the women from outside entered the bathroom and paused for a moment. Joan looked at her and continued to the sink to wash her hands. "Look… I'm sorry, okay? It was a complete accident. I know you're going through a lot right now, and I don't mean to add to your stress. I worked with Daryl and I know you're his daughter. So please, I insist that you let me buy you breakfast." Joan looked at the girl standing behind her in the reflection of the mirror. She was an average-sized woman with long black hair pulled into a ponytail. She had light brown eyes and her name tag said, Marge. Her facial expression gave a look of sincerity. 'Alright, bittie, if you insist…' Thought Joan as she turned around. "Okay, sure. Fine." Said, Joan. "Okay great come on." Said Marge who grew a smile on her face, you could tell the young lady just wanted to be nice and help in any way she could. Once the two women waited in line, they ordered their meals and both sat down in a booth together. "So, I saw you here last night." Said Marge as she dipped a nugget into the sweet and sour sauce. "Yes. I was talking with the fairy godmother and the wicked witch of the west over there behind the counter. I gave them some flyers of my dad." Said Joan as she took a bite out of her snack wrap. Marge laughed at her description of Richard and Janet."I've got to say I like the way you worded that. It was a perfect description." Said Marge as smiled and began to laugh. "Yeah, she isn't the only one I'm not too fond of in this shit hole of a restaurant." Said Joan as she stared at Marge with a fierce look in her eyes. She didn't know one thing about the women. Joan couldn't seem to figure Marge out. "I hear you 100% on that. No matter how much we clean this dump it still looks like a piece of shit. Everyone says it all the time…I mean we do our best but, your father Daryl is the one that keeps this place in one piece." Said, Marge.Joan paused for a moment.'Daddy where are you?' thought Joan. She was trying her best to hide the stress she was feeling, and hearing the women talk about her dad got her thinking. She was thinking even harder than she had been. Joan then shook it off once more and snapped back into reality." Speaking of him…I-I think I need to wrap up here and go." Said Joan as she reached for her phone to check the time. "Oh okay, well listen…If you ever need someone to talk to or just help, you can call me if you'd like?" Said Marge as she stared into Joan's eyes. Joan lost herself for a quick second as she stared into Marge's hazel-colored eyes. She had such long beautiful eyelashes. She almost felt like she could trust Marge, but Joan was not interested in a pity party."Thanks for the offer, I'll keep it in mind…I will get going, thank you for not running me over, and most of all thank you for the free meal." Said Joan as she read 9:30 am on her phone and stood up. "Well take my number if you want?" Said Marge as she pulled out a pen and quickly wrote on a napkin. Suddenly a woman's voice from across the room cut in. "Uh oh, Marge I see you! Trying to get those digits huh?" Said the girl as she walked with a cup in one hand. She was a pretty young black woman with a name tag that read Sheila. "She's a cute girl, go ahead!" Shouted Sheila. 'What is this chick talking about?" Thought Joan as she watched Sheila smile, she gave her and Marge a look as if she knew something was going on.'Why is she looking at us like that? …Get those digits? She's a cute girl, go ahead. What does she mean…oh wait…' Thought Joan who was beginning to realize what Sheila was insinuating. She had an idea that Marge was into women. Could it be? Or was she just overthinking? The question only entered her mind because she was gay. Joan then took another glance. She quickly reached for Marge's number. "Maybe we can get some coffee when I have a chance." Said Joan as she nodded for Marge's assurance. Instantly a smile grew on Marge's face. "Yeah, Just give me a call, I don't bite." Said Marge who now had a sweet and soft tone in her voice. At that moment Joan stepped out of this attraction she began to feel, she looked Marge in her eyes once more. Both their eyes locked in on one another. With each step Joan took backward she couldn't stop staring. "See you later," Said Marge."Bye." Said Joan as she turned around and headed for the exit.

Joan sped down the road and began to slow down as she reached the police station. She pulled into the parking lot, got off her bike, and rushed for the entrance. ``You better be here Officer Thomas…" Thought Joan as she pulled open the glass doors and stepped inside. The station had no one inside the lobby. A glass booth covered the main office. Inside the office were two staff members. One was an older bald man who had the name, Bob. The other was a gorgeous red-headed woman who wore glasses. Slowly Joan proceeded to the glass window."Excuse me?" said Joan. Charlotte looked up with a welcoming smile."Hello, What can I help you with today?" Said Charlotte. Joan tried to fake a smile and replied. "Hi. I'm looking for Detective James Thomas. He's the man I believe is working on trying to locate my father…He's been missing." Charlotte grew a look of compassion and tilted her head to the side. "Oh, I'm so sorry to hear this. Just give me a moment, I'll page him to see if he's in the building." Said Charlotte as she reached for the phone on her desk. "He might be on his lunch break. I think I saw him and Detective Green leave the building not too long ago." Said Bob at the next booth over. "I'm sorry, May I have your name?" Asked Charlotte as she waited for Detective Thomas to answer her call. "My name is Joan Parker." Said Joan when suddenly a man's voice cut in. "Ms. Parker, How are you?" said the voice behind Joan. "Detective Thomas! What a surprise, I was just trying to page you." Said Charlotte as she hung up the phone. Joan turned around and looked to see Detective Thomas standing behind her. The Detective was an average-sized kind of man. He had bright blue eyes and his hair was completely white. He looked to be in his early forties. "Hello, Detective. I wanted to speak with you, about your investigation that involves my father…I can't sit around and not do anything. I want to be able to help in any way possible. If there's anything I can do to help, please tell me. " Said Joan as she looked deeply into Detective Thomas's eyes. "Ms. Parker, the department and I are doing our best to locate your dad's whereabouts. There are steps to take in this process and we are doing so. I can assure you, this case is in good hands. My partner, Detective Green, is setting up times so he can question all the workers that worked with Daryl the night he went missing." Said, Detective Thomas. "Okay, so you're saying, you think it could be someone he worked with that has something to do with this?" asked Joan. "Ms. Parker, it is far too soon for me to give any kind of information, you want facts don't you?" Asked The Detective as he looked Joan hard in the eye. She began to nod the answer yes. "Well as soon as I have some facts or any kind of evidence to go off of. I will personally call you. Until then I need you to relax, get some rest and keep yourself occupied." Said, Detective Thomas. Joan tried to understand, but she began to feel some type of way from the detective's response. 'Relax? Keep me occupied? How the fuck am I supposed to relax?' thought Joan as she folded her arms and became frustrated. "Listen, Detective. I know you mean well, but I can not just "relax" Do you want me to fucking sit back and twiddle my thumbs? I need answers!" Exclaimed Joan as she lost her composure. Detective Thomas grew wide-eyed and looked away for a moment. He then looked Joan in the eyes once more. "Ms. Parker please calm down, I understand you're under—" Joan snapped once more and rudely interrupted the detective. "No, don't tell me to calm down! And don't recite your fucking lines, that you say to everybody else. My father is out there and I need you to hurry up! Please, find him!" Shouted Joan as she pointed and glared at him like she meant business. "Ms. Parker…I will call you. Have a good day." Said Detective Thomas who began to walk away. Joan felt her emotions piercing her body, she had a temper and it just made her make a fool of herself. After realizing how irrational she was acting, Joan brushed it off and began to leave the police station.

Chapter 3 Jessie & Jaylyn

It was 12:30 at night at McDonald's President Ave. had been closed for about an hour now. All of the workers were finally finishing up closing the store. Jessie was the closing manager on the floor for the night and she was exhausted. It was just another boring day she couldn't wait to complete. The only thing that was different about the day was a Detective had stopped by. Detective Green had notified Janet that he wanted to question people who were on the floor the night Daryl went missing. As Jessie processed sales on the computer, she honestly felt bad for the guy. She couldn't stand Daryl. She never liked him. Daryl was a mean smelly and Crank old man. Jessie was surprised someone loved him. The truth was She didn't care if came back or not. "Hey, Jess?" Said, Kelsey. 'Ugh, what does this little bitch want?" Thought Jessie as she put a fake smile on and turned around. "Is it okay if I leave early? Like I know the rules but my dad has to be somewhere early tomorrow and he's already outside. Plus everyone is already clocked out up front." Said Kelsey who was practically begging. Usually, the answer would be no. It was a part of safety rules and regulations that all staff who close the store leave together. Jessie thought about it for a moment."Ahh fuck it…you know what, yes! Everyone can get the hell out actually. I've got an idea for me and Bae tonight' thought Jessie as she began to smile.

She had a plan for her and Jaylyn. "Yes, you can go, and so can everyone else." Said, Jessie. instantly Kelsey grew a smile. "Oh my god! Thanks, Jessie!" said Kelsey as she ran to the front to tell everyone. "You're welcome," Said Jessie as she typed some more sales into the computer. "Jess, the dishes are done, do you need me to do anything else?" Asked Marge as she unclogged the drain to the sink. 'No just get the fuck out' Thought Jessie as her smile grew wider. "No. But do me a favor and tell Jaylyn to come here, then you can go." Said, Jess. Marge began to smile and said, "Okay thanks a lot, have a good night." She then quickly went to grab her bag down in the basement. After closing the system, Jess grabbed her purse to look for a mint. She'd been waiting for Jaylyn to return from the bathroom and now was her chance to spruce up. As she rummaged through her purse she found some perfume by Taylor Swift she'd just bought and sprayed it on. 'Got to smell good for my baby' thought Jessie. She was feeling so tempted to kiss Jaylyn all day long. All she wanted to do was give her man all the love she could give. Jessie wanted to have sex. The thought of his touch made her quiver inside, it was big and he could work it. Suddenly someone grabbed Jessie from behind. "Jesus!" shouted Jessie who was now frightened. "Shh it's me...why are you scared?" Said Jaylyn who was holding Jessie tightly against himself. "Jay! Don't do that! You scared me..." Said Jessie, who began to calm down and feel safe in her man's arms. "Oh, but is it okay if I do this?" Asked Jaylyn as he began to kiss her neck. His lips were soft and wet. He pecked his way up her neck with passionate kisses and licked her as if she was made of sweet candy. "Shit, you know how to kiss the right spots don't you?" Asked Jess as she pressed her ass against his waist. She could feel his cock throbbing like it was a caged animal. Waiting to be unleashed. "You like that shit huh?" Said Jess as he began to move his hands lower to the buttons of her pants. "I fucking love that shit, you know I do." Said Jessie as she turned to kiss her charming prince. Both Jessie and Jaylyn made out passionately until the craving for euphoria became far too strong. Jaylyns hands quickly slipped under her pants and into her panties. His hands were so cold at first but grew warm as he traveled between her legs. "Yes, Daddy..give it to me." Thought Jessie as he rubbed his crotch against her crotch and fondled her left nipple."You want to do something crazy?" Whispered Jay. "I don't know, tell me what you have in mind." Said, Jess."Let's fuck in the play place." Said Jaylyn.

Jessie paused for a moment to process Jaylyn's idea. She wasn't sure if he was serious or not. "What? You're kidding right?" Asked Jessie who was beginning to laugh. "No I'm serious, let's do it." Said Jaylyn as he took his hands out of Jessie's pants and pulled her in the direction out of the grill.

"Jay No! Kids play in there, that's nasty. " Said Jessie as she tried to pull away.` That's the point, it's time to get nasty you dig?" Said Jaylyn as he began to laugh.

Unfortunately, Jessie didn't find it amusing. "Jaylyn no…why do you want to do it in there?" Asked Jessie as she rolled her eyes and refused to budge.

"Because it's sneaky. Don't you feel more turned on when you're trying to sneak?" Asked Jay as he looked into Jessie's eyes. It was something about the way he looked at her; it made her so weak inside. His charming ways and seductive looks made Jessie melt inside. 'Anything you want, just fuck me.' Thought Jessie.

"That look on your face tells me you're coming." Said Jay as he pulled Jessie along with him. She'd finally given in to his idea and began to walk with him out of the grill area. "You're lucky the cheap bastard who owns this store hasn't invested in cameras. " Said, Jessie.

When the couple made it to the entrance of the indoor play place, Jessie reached inside her purse to unlock the door. "You're helping me clean the spot we use when we're done." Said Jessie as she reached into her pocket for the keys and began to unlock the door. "Yeah, yeah, yeah. Just get that ass in there." Said Jaylyn as he smacked Jessie's ass and squeezed it. The play place was a large room. Upon entering there was a Ronald McDonald statue sitting on the bench. Something about the clown always gave Jessie the chills. She took a deep breath and followed Jay to the small steps that lead to the bright yellow tubes. After Descending to the top Jessie followed Jay into the tunnel. "I can't believe we're doing this." Said Jessie as she crawled behind Jaylyn. "You know you love it." Said Jay as he stopped mid-way by one of the plastic windows and laid on his back. "It's so cramped in here. I can't even deal…" Said Jessie who was feeling slightly annoyed. "Why don't you crawl over me and I'll unbutton your top for you?" Suggested Jaylyn.

Jessie smiled and crawled over to her secret lover allowing him to unbutton her blouse. "God, you have such a beautiful set of breasts, I just want to bite them." Said Jay as he nibbled and kissed Jessie's breast. His lips felt so good to Jessie; she loved Jaylynns foreplay. His kisses made her drift away to another place for a moment. Jessie closed her eyes as he began to pull down her pants and pull on her black bra with his teeth. She then opened her eyes and looked outside the window beside her. Suddenly Jessie's heart felt like it skipped a beat. Far off in the distance she randomly spotted a man standing in the room. "Whoa! Wait for a second! Wait! Someone's out there! Shit! Jay look!" whispered Jessie who was trying not to shout as she crawled off Jaylyn. "What? Who the fuck is out there?" whispered Jay as tried to get a better look.

When Jay finally got to peak all there was to be seen was an enormous puddle. It appeared to be grease. "Shit! What the hell is going on? He just dumped grease everywhere" Said Jay who was now infuriated. Jessie's heart now began to race. She didn't understand how someone was standing out there when she locked up the store already. No one was inside the building when she checked earlier. "What the hell is that? I checked all the restrooms. Whoever that is must have broken in here." Said Jessie who was trying her best not to freak out. "Why is there so much grease? Who the fuck does that? You show up and dump grease all over the damn place? You stay here, I'm going down there. " Said Jaylyn as he crawled around Jessie to exit the tubes. "Okay, Just be careful to button my shirt still." Said Jessie as she began to pull her pants back up.

As Jaylyn climbed back down each step his frustration escalated. Once reached the floor he was at a loss for words. The entire puddle they witnessed was somehow gone; it was as if It had evaporated into thin air. "What the…Where did it go?" Asked Jay as he looked all over the floor. Suddenly a noise broke the silence. The sound of something sticky flew up the slide of the play place rapidly. "Jay, what the hell is going on?" Said Jessie as she made her way down the tubes. Suddenly something lunged at her from behind. She let out a scream and felt something with great strength whip her in the opposite direction. Whatever was grabbing Jessie's leg had no mercy.

"What's happening?!" Screamed Jessie as she was battered against the walls of the tubes. Jay suddenly found it harder to breathe. All he could hear was Jesse freaking out and screaming for help. "Jessie what's going on?!" shouted Jay as he ran for the play place. When he approached the steps Jessie came flying out of the slide. Jessie smacked against the floor while screaming and began to crawl. Her nose was bleeding now. "Jay, please help me! There's a monster! We have to run now!" Shouted Jessie as Jay rushed to help her. "What are you saying? What the hell did this to you?!" yelled Jaylyn as he began to help Jessie off the floor and make a run for it. Quickly something flew in the direction of Jay and snatched him away."Jessie help!" Screamed Jay as he was pulled away by the unknown foe. Jessie whipped around to see a blob-like creature. The brown-colored freak looked as if it was made out of some type of liquid. She couldn't believe her eyes as she watched it retract its arm with Jay in its hand. "What do you want? Please just don't hurt him!" Pleaded Jessie as she backed away in fear. She didn't know what to do; she wanted to call 911 but couldn't because she had left her purse back in the grill.

"Please don't kill me!" Begged Jaylyn as he looked face to face with the monster. The creature's face appeared to be melted and unidentifiable. Suddenly the creature roared in anger and smashed Jaylyn into one of the building's support beams face-first. The fatal blow killed Jay before he hit the floor. Jessie then began to cry as she started to run away towards the dining room. As she made it to the door the creature snatched her by the ankle and caused her to fall forward on the floor.

"No!" Screamed Jessie as she was dragged across the floor. She began to scream uncontrollably."Jesus Christ! Please let me go!" Shouted Jessie who was beyond bewildered by what was happening. The monster then quickly crawled over her body. All Jessie could smell was grease as it drooled a brown liquid onto her face. She couldn't stop crying as she lay still before the mutant. "Please. Just let me go…I won't tell anybody, I swear." Cried, Jessie. Slowly the creature began to lean into Jessie as if it wanted a kiss. Jessie's eyes grew wide as she looked away from the monster that had the stench of pure grease. The creature quickly grabbed her by the jaw but Jessie squeezed her mouth shut. She shook her head and cried even harder. Finally, the monster pried her mouth open making Jessie let out a scream. The monster immediately locked lips with Jessie who was now being held down. She started to kick and scream but the creature was much too strong for her to push away. A few seconds later, the creature began to vomit into her mouth. Jessie started to gag as she choked on a constant flow of grease. The liquid kept spewing into her mouth, choking out any scream she let out. As the grease kept flowing Jessie began to vomit. Her legs once kicking began to slow down and come to a stop. While the grease flowed in she was losing oxygen. After 5 minutes Jessie's eyes rolled back and she dropped dead. The grease monster then stopped and stood up over her body. Its entire body began to jerk and fidget. The creature instantly morphed into the shape of Daryl Parker. His entire body was molded into the shape of which he used to be. The monster was now the shape of a man dragging Jessie's dead body.

Chapter 4 Marge and Joan

It was a stressful afternoon for Marge as she drove inside her blue Honda Civic. She and her brother Charles had another fight. All the drama was about her smoking cigarettes in the house. She didn't know why she still smoked and Charles hated the fact that she did. Smoking was the reason why their mom was dead. The way he went off on her made her get up and leave the house. If smoking didn't relieve the stress then she turned to weed. Before her eight-hour shift, she planned to meet up with her co-worker Sheila for a quick fix. As Marge drove down the street she eventually reached the mini downtown area of Fall River. Traffic was packed at the stoplight and it was delaying her from reaching Sheila on time, she was already 10 minutes late. Though Sheila tried to act like she was Marge's friend, Marge knew the things she would say behind her back. She had a feeling Sheila was going to be dogging her about being late once again. Sheila had this big talk about how good her man's weed was. She was also the only one who answered Marge's text message, here Marge was driving to pay Sheila for weed. Finally, after turning left at the intersection Marge drove down a hill. She was headed for the park by the boardwalk called battleship cove. Sheila had told Marge to meet her and her boyfriend Ben in the parking lot. As Marge pulled up to the scene she could see Ben and Sheila waiting. Sheila was sitting outside the car wearing short shorts and a pink belly button top. She also was rocking shades. Ben was a skinny white man with a buzz cut and rocking shades. 'Alright, let's do this." Thought Marge as she pulled a twenty dollar bill out of her pocket. Slowly Marge pulled into the parking lot beside Sheila's car. "Hey girl, how are you?" Asked Sheila. "Hey Sheila, I'm okay and you?" asked Marge who grew a small smile. "You know how it is girl, I'm just out here in this heat waiting on you. What took you so long? You stay late, girl." Said Sheila as she walked closer to Marge's window and discretely dropped a bag in the car. "I know, it was the traffic though. It drives me nuts how badly people drive around here." Said Marge as she popped the twenty up for Sheila to grab it. "Damn, well next time plan shit ahead. You stay using excuses. People got things to do, people to see and places to be." Said Sheila as she snatched the twenty from Marge's hand. "Sorry." Said Marge who didn't care what Sheila had to say. "Nah it's whatever though, just work on that shit okay? By the way, my man told me the shit you got is called Loud. Your Lesbo ass is going to love it" Said Sheila as she looked at her acrylic nails and proceeded to walk away without saying goodbye, quickly Marge started her car feeling enraged by Sheila's comment. 'Lesbo ass? How disrespectful!' thought Marge. "Hey Sheila!" Shouted Marge as she backed away. Sheila slowly turned around and stopped before she opened her door. "Fuck you!" screamed Marge as she flipped her middle finger out the window and quickly put her car in reverse." I know she did not just, oh hell no! fuck you too bitch! Come say that shit to my face! You fucking nasty ass! bipolar! lesbian cunt!"

Shouted Sheila as she flipped her middle finger back at Marge who was already speeding out of the parking lot.

Marge drove down the road feeling skeptical. She didn't know how she let that happen. Marge was tired of taking shit from people and she guessed Sheila's comment was what finally set her off. After denying several of Sheila's attempts to call her she tried to forget about it. It was time to focus on how she was about to get high out of her mind. Eventually, she reached a 7-11 and pulled into the parking lot, when her cell phone began to ring. Marge checked the number to only see it was a number she'd never seen before. "Stop calling me Sheila!" Answered Marge."Whoa, hold on. This is Joan!" Said the voice over the phone. Marge's jaw dropped in shock. She felt extremely embarrassed. "Oh my god! Joan, I am so sorry. I thought this was someone else."Said, Marge. Joan began to laugh at Marge's response."It's fine. Don't worry about it. I assume someone was blowing up your phone."Said, Joan."Yeah, I had a little incident. Anyway, what's up? How are you?" Asked Marge who was trying to divert Joan from finding out why she answered the phone as she did."I uh, was just wondering if you wanted to get that coffee if you weren't busy today." Said Joan with a nervous voice. Marge smiled. Joan's voice was such a turn-on. "No, I'm free right now. I've got work later on but we can still hang out." "Okay, sounds great. I'll meet you at the Dunkin Donuts near your job. " Said, Joan."Sounds great, I'll see you soon." Said, Marge."See you later, bye." Said, Joan. After they both hung up, Marge headed for the 7-11 to grab some wraps for the weed.'She's so smoking with me." Thought Marge.

Joan Stood outside Dunkin Donuts and began to smoke a cigarette as she daydreamed. She felt like couldn't be alone and needed some company to keep the worry she felt off her mind. A few minutes later a horn honked twice making Joan snap back into reality. It was Marge pulling in. She stopped the car and stepped out. She wore a tight black shirt with blue denim jeans and white sneakers. She was looking cute."Hey Joan." Said marge with an enthusiastic tone in her voice. "Hello Marge, it's nice to see you." Said, Joan. "It's nice to see you too. Especially Under better circumstances as well." Said, Marge. "Yeah, let's just forget about the whole car thing. Let's start fresh okay?" Asked Joan who was trying to smile."That's fine, I'm glad you feel this way." Said Marge as she walked with Joan and opened the door for her to enter the restaurant. After ordering two coffees the two women both sat down by a window. Joan picked up her coffee and blew at the steam that drifted from the lid."So why are you so nice to me Marge?" Asked Joan as she sipped from the hot coffee. Marge looked as if she didn't know how to answer the question. "Well I'm generally a nice girl, I just wanted to reach out to you." Said Marge as she took a sip from her latte. "You don't even know me, and you're buying me coffee. I feel like we're on a date." Said Joan as she smiled and sipped some more."I never said this was a date. Did you want this to be a date?" Asked Marge as she locked eyes with Joan. 'Maybe I do…' Thought Joan as she lost herself once again in Marge's hazel eyes. Joan Laughed and looked away. "I'm going to be real open with you. I kind of thought you were gay after meeting you." Said, Joan. Marge suddenly sipped her coffee too fast and coughed in reaction to what Joan said.

"What made you think that?" asked Marge who had a look of concern as she cleared her throat. Joan smiled and sipped her coffee some more. "Your co-worker in the restaurant gave me the idea when she was talking to you and gawking at us." Said, Joan. "Wow…well I'll be really honest with you. Yes. I'm gay, I also think you're a beautiful woman and I want to get to know you." Said Marge as she took another sip of coffee. "Hmm…I think that doesn't sound like a bad idea." Said Joan as she smiled even more. "I agree…so I was wondering with all this stress you've got going on, what are you doing to relax? I know you've got to be worried sick." Said, Marge. "Well I just try to keep myself busy, I work at the library so I'm there most of the day." Said Joan. "Have you ever smoked weed?" asked Marge. 'Wow, she just asked me that.' Thought Joan who looked like she was giving her next response thought. "I used to. It's been a long, long time since the last time I picked up a blunt. Why do you ask?" Asked Joan as she sat back. "I've got a blunt rolled in my car. Why don't you come smoke with me before we split?" Asked Marge as she leaned forward to drink some coffee. "I don't know." Said, Joan. "Come on it'll be fun, you looked stressed out. Let me help you out okay?" Asked Marge who was waiting for the word yes to come out of Joan's mouth. 'I can't believe she wants to smoke…Maybe it won't be such a bad thing.' Thought Joan as she began to nod. "Okay let's go." Said Joan who was starting to smile. "Great, I'm glad you said yes. I've got some loud in the car." Said Marge as she stood up and got ready to leave. Joan then grabbed her coffee and followed the wild woman out the door. The two pretty women hopped inside Marge's car ready for a good time. Marge started her car and passed the blunt to Joan as she began to pull out."My god that shit smells beautiful." Said Joan as she sniffed the blunt.

"You like that smell don't ya?" Asked Marge who was growing excited as Joan sparked the blunt. 'Oh yeah that that's the fucking stuff.' thought Joan as she let the smoke fill her lungs. The high was phenomenal, she felt her state of mind changes instantly. After enjoying her two hits. She passed the blunt to Marge as she drove down the road. Marge Slowly drove through the city with a feeling of relaxation, Joan was in her zone as she grooved to Justin Timberlake's song T.K.O."So, you're enjoying the smoke I see." Said Marge as she turned another corner. She was taking Joan on a blunt ride and driving aimlessly around the neighborhood. "Hell yes." Said Joan as she passed the blunt to Marge. "Good, I'm glad I could help." Said, Marge. Slowly Joan stretched her arm around Marge's seat. "So why don't you pull over?" Asked Joan. Marge felt Joan's vibe telling her that pulling over was a magnificent idea. Quickly she pulled over to an empty Parking lot. "Why do you want me to pull over?" Asked Marge, already knowing the answer."Because I've been dying to do this." Said Joan as she reached in and kissed Marge. Joan's lips were soft and felt wonderful as they locked onto Marge's. She'd been waiting to steal a kiss the minute she felt the high take over her mind. As they kissed Marge let her tongue travel and play with Joan's. Each second the more intense the make-out session became. As the two women kissed one another, Joan began to rub her hand against Marge's breast. 'Fuck that feels good.' Thought Marge as her hand moved deeper into Joan's thigh. Joan then began to play with Marge's nipples as she kissed her more and more. The way Joan was touching Marge made her so wet. All she wanted to do was eat Joan out. "Can I eat that for you?" Said Marge as her hand traveled down between Joan's legs. Marge then spread her legs and let Joan rub her crotch as she groped Joan's breast. "Wait…" Said, Joan. "What's wrong?" asked Marge. Joan slowly pulled away. "I don't think we should be doing this." Said, Joan. Marge nodded and pulled away from the beautiful young woman. "How come?" asked Marge who was feeling like she'd been teased. "I just think you should come over tonight…after you get out of work, I mean I so want to fuck, but not here. Not in public." Said Joan who was trying to be as nice as possible. "You're right…I just got so caught up in the way that you were kissing me. You do it so well." Said Marge who was overwhelmed with temptation. Not only did she want to kiss those soft lips on her face, but she also wanted to feel Joan's warm embrace. Coming over sounded like a brilliant idea. "So tonight, I'll be outside when you get off work. When you're all set, come out and follow me home." Marge smiled and said, "Sounds like a plan to me."

Chapter 5 Detective Green

Detective Ryan Green sat in the divided Section of the play place waiting patiently. He was a stocky red-headed man in his late 40's. He had a long afternoon of work, he'd finally found his way inside Mcdonald's President Avenue. The detective had been inside the building for most of the afternoon questioning some of the workers. They were on the floor the night Daryl Parker had gone missing. He'd come in at 3 pm and spoke with four different employees. Each of the workers had worked with Daryl the night he went missing. All Detective Green needed to do was question three more people out of the four he had crossed off his list.

The detective needed to speak with Marge Peterson, Jessie McBride, and Jaylyn Sousa. It was brought to Detective Green's attention by Janet the store manager that both Jessie and Jaylyn wouldn't be in until the next day. All that was left on the interrogation list for the day was Marge Peterson. Ten minutes had passed when Janet came to the glass doors of the play place and entered with Marge Peterson. She was about ten minutes late. As she stepped into the divided section alone the detective looked at her carefully. She had a blank facial expression as she approached the table Detective Green was sitting at.

"Good afternoon ms. Peterson. How are you?" Asked Green as he stood up and tried to shake Marge's hand.

Marge looked at Detective Green's hand for a moment and shook it. "Hello, Detective…what can I do for you today?" Asked Marge as she sat down. "I just had a few questions for you in regard to Mr. Daryl Parker. To my understanding, you were on the floor with several other employees the night he went missing." Said, Green.
"That's correct." Said, Marge. "Do you know if anyone had any problems with Mr. Parker?" Asked Detective Green. Marge sat and thought for a minute. "Detective, I'm going to be real honest with you, Daryl isn't exactly everyone's favorite around here. In fact, most people can't stand him because he's so grumpy all the time. The guy was just mean." Said, Marge. "I see. You know it's funny you say this because everyone that I have spoken with has an answer worse or similar to your response. The guy wasn't very popular around here huh?" Asked Detective Green as he added some notes to his report. "Well he was popular…but not in any way you and I would like to be. A lot of people would crack jokes about his hygiene, or his short temper. His language was atrocious too. The minute the guy was ticked off he sounded worse than a sailor." Said, Marge. The Detective nodded his head and looked into Marge's eyes like he was staring into her soul. She seemed like she had nothing to hide. "So Marge, out of everyone. Were you any of the employees that participated in Teasing or harassing Mr. Parker?" Asked Detective Green. Marge's eyes grew wide as she shook her head to answer no. "No, no I didn't. If anything I was always nice to the man. I just try to mind my business around here." Said, Marge. "Okay. And on that night, did you see any kind of suspicious activity going on outside? Anyone in the parking lot before you and your co-workers left the store?"

Asked Detective Green."Nope. No, I can't say I saw anything unusual." Said, Marge. "Okay. Well, Ms. Peterson, That's all I need from you for this afternoon. You may return to the floor, thank you for your time." Said Detective Green as he closed his notebook and looked to see 6 pm on his silver wristwatch. "Okay, have a good day, and good luck with this investigation. I hope you find him." Said Marge as she began to back away.

"Thank you, Ms. Peterson. I hope we find him too." Said Detective Green as he followed the young women out of the play place.

Chapter 6 The shift of events

Marge quickly rushed down the hall of the basement. She was frustrated because she left her hat at home; the only solution was a box full of paper hats that were supplied for workers in Marge's predicament. When She arrived in the room, Richard was using the designated computer for managers only. "Hey Margie, how are you?" Asked Richard as he began to sip on his coffee. "Hi, Richard." Said Marge as she reached up for the box of gloves on a nearby shelf. "Isn't it a shame with what's happened to poor Daryl?" Said Richard as he stood to grab some papers he was printing out. "Yes, it's terrible." Said, Marge. "I know, it sucks. If we don't find him we are going to have to hire someone else. I don't want to sound like an ass, but Daryl sucked balls at cleaning. He was too old and he was an ass hole." Said, Richard. "Wow, that's nice of you to say." Said Marge who was feeling shocked and almost wanted to laugh at how random Richard sounded. "I'm sorry. Honestly, I hope the guy is found, but I'm trying to convince Janet to hire someone else. That way when the guy retires. We're much younger. Faster and more efficient backup." Said Richard.``How can you already be planning his replacement? The guy has been gone for over a week." Said, Marge. She didn't like the way Richard was speaking about Joan's father. "Whoa, look at you getting all defensive. Calm down, sweetheart! Wait for a second, I know what this is about". The flamboyant Richard's eyes grew wider, and then said. "I heard Sheila say you and his daughter were hooking up the other day." Marge rolled her eyes, 'Fucking Sheila,' She thought as she looked Richard up and down. She wasn't surprised that everyone knew about her business, because rumors spread like wildfire in this establishment. "We were not hooking up, I was just trying to be nice to the girl and we became friends." Said, Marge. Richard smiled and laughed. "Oh yeah? I know how that goes. My boyfriend and I were just "Friends" at first. You don't have to lie sweetie. She's gay isn't she?" Asked Richard. He was far too interested in other people's business. Marge knew he was one of the people who spread rumors.``That's none of your business." Said Marge as she placed a white paper hat on her head. Quickly Marge rushed out of the room when she noticed Grease seeping outside the door. "Great! Richard, there is grease seeping from the cracks in the ceiling." Said, Marge. Quickly Richard walked over to see grease on the floor.``It's been doing that in different spots of the restaurant all day long. We can't figure out why." Said Richard who now looked frustrated. Marge looked at the puddle on the floor. She realized she wasn't seeing things the other day.``I'll go get the mop." Said, Marge. After several hours it finally reached a certain time of night. It was closing time, and it was time for everyone to prepare to clean the store. "Marge!" Shouted Janet. Quickly Marge came running around the corner with a broom in her hand. "Yes, Janet?" Asked Marge.Janet glared at Marge. She always had a mean mug on her face, it made anyone's mood drop. "I need you to get a mop for another leak from the ceiling! It's coming faster than usual so I need you to hurry." Said Janet as she investigated the growing puddle on the floor. As Marge headed for the mop she looked up at the ceiling, it looked to be in the worst condition she'd ever seen. "Oh my god, what's up with the ceiling?" Said Tracey, who had several other workers behind her to get a look at the scene. "Everyone needs to stand clear from the ceiling! It's not safe." Said Richard as he made his way past everyone. He couldn't stop staring at the severity of how damaged the ceiling was becoming.``I don't understand how all this grease dripped from the ceiling. It doesn't make sense! How is this happening?" Said Janet as she pondered at the crackling ceiling. She then grew an idea.``Geo, can you come here?" Asked Janet. Immediately Geo was squeezed by Kelsey and Tracey. "Yes, Janet?" Asked Geo. "Help Richard move this table so my microwave doesn't get grease all over it." Ordered Janet who was starting to panic. Geo looked at the ceiling and looked at all the grease. His eyes widened, he didn't want to be anywhere near the ceiling. "But Janet, I think the ceilings are going to cave in." Said Geo as he slowly approached the table."Oh just do it!" said Janet in the rudest way possible. Geo nodded and positioned himself to help Richard push the table out of the way. "Okay little man, let's do this." Said, Richard. Geo stared at Richard for a moment with a dirty look. He then began to help move the table out of the space.Quickly Marge came running with the mop bucket when suddenly debris from the ceiling came crashing down onto the microwave. Instantly what appeared to be a fountain of grease came spewing out. All the grease in the hole splashed all over Richard and Geo. "What the fuck!" Screamed Geo who was now angry that he was drenched in grease."How could this happen!?" Shouted Janet who was in shock to see the floor smothered in grease. "Oh my god! It's in my hair!" Screamed Richard as he wiped the grease off his face.Suddenly a hand rose from the grease and swept Geo off his feet. The small man flew backward on the floor letting out a scream."Oh my god, everyone saw that right?" Asked Marge. She thought she was seeing things, but everyone in the room had seen the hand. They all gasped in astonishment. Everyone felt unsure of what they had just seen."See what?" Asked Richard as he whipped grease from his eyes. At that moment the grease rose up and quickly morphed into a figure. Richard gasped and began to scream like a woman the moment he could see the creature rise. "What the fuck is that!" Screamed Kelsey. Suddenly at the speed of light, the grease monster slammed the metal table forward. The force was so strong that it sent Richard flying against the wall. "What the hell is that thing!" Screamed Richard. It was within a few seconds later that Geo began to crawl away in horror as he watched all the grease begin to transform into a greasy figure that stood on its hind legs. "What in God's name is that!?" Shouted Janet who had Marge, Tracey, and Kelsey standing behind her. The creature then let out a scream as it slammed the sharp-edged table into Richard. Instantly Richard was cut in half. All hell broke loose as his lower abdomen fell to the floor and spewed blood everywhere. He then began to cough up blood. Richard's facial expression grew dazed and confused as his legs fell to the floor. He couldn't process anything as he leaned on the microwave and his intestines dangled below him. "Run!" Screamed Tracey who was beginning to run with everyone else in the opposite direction. Marge quickly ran to the front counter and smashed into the metal ice container, she lost balance and hit the floor. As Marge began to get up Janet came wobbling behind her. "I'm not dying damn it! Fuck all of you!" Screamed Janet when suddenly she slipped on the ice and fell on the floor. Behind Janet came Tracey and Kelsey running around the corner. Suddenly a long hand stretched behind them and snatched Kelsey away."NO! Tracey help me!" Screamed Kelsey as she was pulled away to her doom.

Tracey whipped around and began to back away in fear. Immediately she reached down and began to help Janet off the floor with Marge. "Let's get the fuck out of here!" Shouted Janet as she began to limp away with Marge and Tracey as support. The women quickly ran for the front exit when surprised by the creature as it crawled across the ceiling and jumped in front of them."Wrong way!" screamed Marge. All three of the women turned around and ran in the direction of the back door. As they ran down the straight way Janet was suddenly snatched away. "No!!" screamed Janet as the creature's arm retracted with Janet in its hands. Instantly the creature snapped her neck and threw her through the ceiling. "She's a goner! Let's go!" Yelled Tracey as she ran with Marge to the back door. 'What is that thing?!' Thought Marge. When the women made it to the emergency exit. They felt a loss of hope. The worktable had been tossed in front of the back door. There was no time to evade the grease monster. Suddenly the monster snatched Tracey and threw her so hard, she flew to the front of the restaurant letting out one final shriek before she landed."Shit! Oh my god! Please! Just leave me alone!" Begged Marge as she backed away. With each step she took, the creature grew closer and closer.

Suddenly the monster screamed as if it was in horrible pain. The liquid on the floor was making the grease monster's feet sizzle. Marge grew confused and spotted a knocked-over bottle of Degreaser on the floor. 'Degreaser? This thing doesn't seem to like it.' Thought Marge. Having no time, she quickly grabbed the bottle and splashed the last of the degreaser into the monster's face. The monster howled in horrible pain as its face burned and sizzled. "Fuck you! You freak!" Screamed Marge as she turned on the soap dispenser over the sink and grabbed the hose. "Take that!" Yelled Marge as she began to douse the monster in hot soapy water. The creature began to scream and grow enraged as it backed away. Finally having a free chance to run, Marge quickly squeezed by the table that blocked the exit. She sprinted down the staircase running for her life. Upon reaching the basement she could hear the grease monster thirst to kill her. Marge knew he had a chance of escaping if she could get out of the building through the storm doors. Having no time to think, she ran for the doors and crawled up the mini ladder. Marge desperately began to unlatch the locks on the doors. "Come on! Come on!" Yelled Marge as she used all her might to push the doors open. After one more push, the storm doors popped open. Quickly Marge pulled herself out of the restaurant. She was now in the back of the store behind the carrel. 'Freedom!' Thought Marge as she ran for the parking lot as fast she could.

When She reached the parking lot she grabbed her cell phone so she could call 911. Suddenly Joan pulled into the parking lot on her motorcycle. "Joan! Please help me!" Screamed Marge as she approached Joan. "Whoa! What's wrong? Are you okay?" Asked Joan as she got off her bike and looked shocked to see Marge outside.

"You wouldn't believe me if I told you. A fucking monster killed everyone inside! It's after me now!" shouted Marge as she began to cry. "A Monster? What are you saying?" Asked Joan who was confused by Marge's response. "I'm not fooling around! This thing just came out of nowhere and murdered everyone!" Yelled Marge as she waited for 911 to answer her call. Suddenly a police car entered the parking lot. "Here come the cops." Said, Joan. "How are they already here?" Asked Marge as she hung up her phone.

"Well I'll be damned, it's Detective Thomas. And Detective Green." Said, Joan. Quickly the car pulled over beside Marge and Joan. "What's going on here? We Just got a call about a monster. Attacking everyone in the restaurant? We thought it was a prank call." Said Detective Green in the driver's seat. "Yes! It's true! There's some sort of freak inside there! It killed everyone!" Shouted Marge. Both the officers looked at Marge with blank facial expressions. They didn't know how to respond to her confirmation.

"Ladies, I'm going to have to ask you to wait inside this vehicle. We're going to check it out." Said Detective Thomas as he stepped out of the car.

"Okay, but the detective who called you? How did you know you came here?" Asked Marge. "Someone locked themselves in the fridge in the basement and called 911." Said Detective Green. "What the hell is going on?" Asked Joan as she got in the back seat of the car with Marge. "You two just wait here and let us handle this." Said Detective Thomas as he pulled out his nine-millimeter and headed for the Mcdonald's restaurant. "Wait! Detectives before you go! I-I know it sounds crazy but that, that thing! It seems to hate Degreaser! It's like he's made out of grease!" Shouted Marge. Detective Green and Thomas both paused and looked at Marge like she was crazy. Slowly Detective Green shut the door. "When we get back we're checking that loony tune for drugs." Said Detective Green as he pulled out his gun and followed Detective Thomas.

Chapter 7 The Grease Monster

The detectives slowly approached the building with caution. They were ready for a hostile situation and both the detectives were prepared. When the Detectives reached the entrance they discovered the doors were locked due to the store being closed already."Great it's fucking locked." Said Detective Thomas as he pulled at the door. "Well, we've got to find a way in." Said detective Green. Suddenly a bloody hand smacked against the dining room window. "Shoot the door open!" Shouted Detective Green. At that moment Detective Thomas shot the door. Shards of glass sprayed to the floor just before he reached in and unlocked the door. Cautiously both the detectives moved inside. "Help me…" Said a young woman that lay in one of the booths. She had brunette hair and blue eyes. Her name tag said, Tracey. The girl seemed to be very dazed and confused. She had a head injury that was leaking blood all over herself. "Jesus! Ryan called an ambulance now!" Said, Detective Thomas."I'm on it." Said Detective Green, Detective Thomas then began to give aid to Tracey and helped her sit up. "Ms. How do you feel? Are you able to stand?" Asked Detective Thomas as he examined how severe her head trauma was. "My head is killing me…" Said Tracy as she wobbled back and forth. "Who did this to you?" Asked detective Thomas. Suddenly a large creek came from the ceiling and a body came crashing down to the table. "Jesus!" Screamed Detective Green. He stopped his phone call and stood in complete shock."Oh my god, it's Janet." Said, Tracy. She quickly stumbled out of the booth and fell into Detective Thomas's arms. Tracey then fell unconscious again. "What is going on?!" shouted Detective Green. "Tell them to hurry up with the ambulance." Said Detective Thomas as he laid Tracey back down. "This is Officer Ryan Green, I need some paramedics over to 1690 President Ave. Immediately. We've got two people in critical condition!" Said Detective Green as he spoke into his radio."Ryan, this woman is dead…I'm not getting any pulse." Said Detective Thomas as he felt Janet's main artery. The detective then reached for his radio as well. "This is Officer James Thomas requesting back up to 1690 Mcdonald's president ave. Immediately, I repeatedly requested backup for a hostile situation at 1690 McDonald's President Ave." Said, Detective Thomas. Quickly Detective Thomas put his radio down and pulled out his gun. He then headed towards the back of the restaurant to investigate the rest of the crime scene. "You bring Ms. Tracey outside. Please keep her safe. I'll be fine." Said Detective Thomas as he walked past Detective Green. "You got it." Said Detective Green.

It was with each step that Detective Thomas took, fear for what else was to come fled all through his mind. As he aimed his gun forward he examined his surroundings. Tons of Cheeseburger wrappers and condiments were spread all over the floor. At the end of the straightaway, there was a knocked-over bun rack blocking his path. He also noticed a table tossed in front of the emergency exit.

'What in God's name happened here?' Thought Detective Thomas. He then cut into the other section of the kitchen that was divided by another table. Once Detective Thomas made it to side two he approached the grilling area. The closer he got to the grill the more he smelt a stench of burning hair and overcooked meat. 'What is that terrible smell?' Thought Detective Thomas as he turned the corner. The next thing he saw made him stop dead in his tracks. A headless corpse lay on the floor with a pool of blood. The decapitated girl's name tag read Kelsey. As Detective Thomas's eyes widened he then noticed her head was smashed to bits over the grill. The girl's brains were literally cooking. He then noticed another pool of blood that led to Richard, Another Manager. He was leaning behind the microwave. The closer Detective Thomas got to the corpse, the more clear Richard's lower half was sliced off and on the floor. "My God!" Exclaimed the Detective as he covered his mouth in shock. Detective Thomas began to back away. He knew he had to check the basement so he aimed his gun forward and rushed away from the gruesome scene. When the Detective reached the staircase, he squeezed by the table that blocked the emergency exit. Once he descended the stairs, he reached the basement. The Freezer and Fridge were across from one another and were the first set of doors seen. Detective Thomas attempted to open the Fridge but the door was locked from the inside. He banged on the door hoping for an answer. "Is there anyone here? This is Officer Thomas from the Fall River police department." "Yes I'm in here I called the Police! I'm coming out!" Said a man's voice. Quickly the detective stepped to the side with his gun positioned at the door. The refrigerator door swung open and a small black man came walking out. His nametag read Geo. "Geo, I'm going to need you to come with me." Said, Detective Thomas."Thank god you're here! That monster was fucking everybody up! My pleasure let's go." Said, Geo. As the Detective began to close the door, Geo stumbled back in shock. "Shit man! Look behind you!" Screamed Geo as he backed away. The Detective whipped around to see a naked man standing three feet away. His body was completely brown, yet it had the face of Daryl Parker. The man was a mold of some sort. "Put your hands in the air and get down on the ground!" Ordered Detective Thomas as he aimed his gun at the unknown Creature."Fuck this shit man!" Screamed Geo as he ran for the Stairs in the opposite direction. Suddenly the man's skin began to stretch and move. His body began to melt and expand as he let out a scream like a monster. With no hesitation, Detective Thomas fired two shots piercing the creature in the head. The creature paused for a moment when the bullet holes began to smoke and burst into flames. "What the hell are you?!" Asked the Detective as he began to fire more bullets into the relentless monster. The creature still continued its pursuit and cornered Detective Thomas. The Detective continued shooting, each shot made the monster howl and back away. The flames grew wilder, its body soon engulfing the creature's entire body. Detective Thomas quickly started to back away, firing more shots. He then made a run for it up the stairs. The detective could hear the monster howling in pain. Its voice echoed up the stairs behind him. Detective Thomas then grabbed the table in front of the fire escape, he immediately swung it in the direction of the stairs. The table then slid down and blocked the monster's path. The Detective then pulled the fire alarm and ran outside.Marge sat inside the police car holding Joan's hand. She could feel her pulse pumping through her hand. Though she was stressed she was relieved to see Geo and Tracey had made it out of the building alive. The fact that any of this had happened was surreal. Monsters weren't supposed to exist. They were supposed to live in sci-fi movies. Comic books! Or Fairytales. It all just didn't seem to click in Marge's mind. All she could think was 'Is this a nightmare? Am I even awake?' A moment later Detective Thomas came sprinting out from behind the restaurant. "Shit, he actually made it!" Shouted Geo who was standing outside with Detective Green."My god! I am glad to see you! I thought you were a goner." Said Detective Green"I will be a goner if we get the hell out of here now!" Shouted Detective Thomas as he hopped inside the car. "You! Cram your ass inside!" Yelled Detective Green as he pointed at Geo and opened the back door.Quickly Geo hopped inside and lay across Tracey, Joan, and Marge's laps. The Detective then rushed to the front seat and got in. "Is there really a monster in there detective? What is it?" Asked Joan. The detective paused for a moment. He didn't know how to answer the question. "I don't know how to tell you…but in one moment, the thing that I saw in there. It looked like it was your father." Said The Detective as he began to back the car away. Joan suddenly couldn't speak. All she could do was cry. "How can you say that's my dad? You're really telling me my dad killed all those people?" Asked Joan. "He ain't making the shit up! I saw his face too. It was Daryl." Said, Geo. Marge held Joan's hand even tighter and tried to comfort her. "It's okay Joan…everything's going to be fine." Said Marge as she rested her head against Joan's. "Has Tracey woken up yet?" Asked Detective Thomas."No, not yet." Said Detective Green."Here it comes! Shit man, look at that thing!" shouted Detective Green. The Grease monster was a complete inferno as it came charging out from behind the restaurant. "Oh my god! What the fuck is that thing!" Shouted Tracey who was just waking up.Quickly Detective Thomas began to back away, suddenly several police cars came pouring into the parking lot with their sirens blaring. "Thank god!" Shouted Marge who felt a huge weight lifted off her chest. Both The Detectives immediately jumped out of their car and began to open fire. "Die you piece of shit!" screamed Detective Thomas as he constantly shot the monster. "Alright boys let him have it! James got back inside the car now!" Shouted Detective Green.Detective Thomas looked at Detective Thomas with many questions on his face but decided to listen. Once they both got back inside, a few moments later the entire police force on duty began throwing water balloons at the creature. The monster began to howl in horrible pain as its body burned and sizzled. The creature was starting to disintegrate. "What's going on? Why are they throwing water balloons at it?!" Asked Detective Thomas."While you were inside I took Ms. Peterson's advice about the Degreaser and ordered them all to bring water balloons filled with the stuff. It was a risk, but I am glad I listened." Said Detective Green as he pulled out his cell phone. He was now recording the monster's Demise. The Grease monster began to ooze and droop down into a muddy goop. "It's working!" shouted Geo. Joan then began to lean closer and get a better look. Suddenly the water balloons stopped flying across the parking lot. In its final moments, the creature melted to the ground. "Detective let me out of the car!" Shouted Joan.Detective Thomas thought for a moment and got out of the car. He quickly rushed over to open the door to grant Joan's request. Joan then let go of Marge's hand and stepped out of the car. As Joan got closer to the defeated creature, all she could smell was degreaser and burnt grease. 'This thing can not be you, Dad...Please you're all I've got.' Thought Joan as she walked with Detective Thomas who had his gun ready to fire. The creature's face was the only thing recognizable in the brown goop. "Daddy is that you?" Asked Joan as she looked down at the monster. The creature slowly looked at Joan and morphed its face into what looked like Daryl."No. NO! Why did you do this!? What happened to you?!" Screamed Joan as she burst into tears. She knew it was her father. "Ms. Parker I don't think you should see him like this..." Said, Detective Thomas. Joan stared at the melting creature and watched it groan in pain. "I love you..." Said Joan as she stood frozen unable to move. "Detective. Please. Let me put him out of his misery...please. Let me have your gun." Asked Joan. Detective Thomas stared long and hard at Joan. He decided to give her the gun. "Whoa! What's going on?" Asked Detective Green who noticed his partner gave her his gun. "Don't worry about it." Said, Detective Thomas. Joan took a deep breath and aimed the gun straight at the groaning creature's head. She didn't want to see him like this any longer; Joan took another breath and pulled the trigger several times, splattering the monster's head to pieces. As she watched the grease smoke up, she now knew her father was free. All that could be seen as a Rock of some sort glowing inside the grease. Joan handed Detective Thomas his gun back and began to walk back to the car. After a night of tragic events, it was finally over. Marge could hear the fire department and ambulances pouring into the parking lot. News stations were now pulling in and reporting what was happening. "Are you okay?" Asked Marge, who was out of the car. "I don't know," Said Joan.Quickly she walked to Marge and began to hug her. Joan needed someone to comfort her. "Everything's going to be just fine…I'll take care of you. Do you hear me? Don't you worry?" Said, Marge. Joan stood with Marge for a long moment and closed her eyes while she stood in her arms. Paramedics then came rushing over to help Tracey out of the car. Firefighters pulled close to the Mcdonald's that was now on fire and rushed to contain the disaster. It was all over. It was finally over.

.

www.ingramcontent.com/pod-product-compliance
Lightning Source LLC
La Vergne TN
LVHW091129180726
843490LV00008B/2901